ADVENTURE IN BEGGAR'S CANYON

By Jane Mason
Illustrated by Gary Ciccarelli

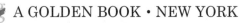 A GOLDEN BOOK • NEW YORK

Golden Books Publishing Company, Inc., New York, New York 10106

®, ™ & © 1998 Lucasfilm Ltd. Title and character and place names protected by all applicable trademark laws. All rights reserved. Used under authorization. Printed in the U.S.A. A GOLDEN BOOK®, A LITTLE GOLDEN BOOK®, G DESIGN™, and the distinctive gold spine are trademarks of Golden Books Publishing Company, Inc. Library of Congress Catalog Card Number: 97-76908 ISBN: 0-307-98879-1   First Edition 1998   A MCMXCVIII

It was a troubled time. An evil Galactic Empire ruled the galaxy, while a band of brave Rebels fought for freedom.

On the outskirts of the galaxy was a planet called Tatooine. Far away from just about everything, this hot desert world was home to only a few creatures and a small population of humans . . . including a teenager named Luke Skywalker.

Luke lived and worked on a moisture farm with his Aunt Beru and his Uncle Owen. They collected moisture from the air and sold it to other desert dwellers.

Luke loved his aunt and uncle, but farming wasn't for him. More than anything, Luke longed for adventure.

One day, Luke and his friend Windy set out for a remote area of Tatooine called Beggar's Canyon. "Let's go target a few womp rats," suggested Luke as they climbed into his T-16 skyhopper. Finally, a day of fun!

Luke steered toward Beggar's Canyon and the skyhopper zoomed over the sands of Tatooine. The rocky walls of the canyon rose in front of them, and soon the two boys were dodging the craggy peaks.

"Yahoo!" Windy cried over the wind.

As the skyhopper shot around a corner, Luke's eyes widened. They had reached a sharp turn! Luke swerved hard to the left, but the skyhopper crashed into a rocky wall!

In a burst of flame, the skyhopper fell to the canyon floor.

"Are you alright?" Luke called as they climbed out of the wreckage.

"I think so," Windy replied shakily.

Luckily, nobody was seriously hurt.

After catching his breath, Luke examined the skyhopper. "This thing'll never fly," he said with a groan.

Luke looked around at the canyon walls. They were miles from help. The canyon was a giant maze of rocky spires. And they didn't have any food with them.

"I've got a bad feeling about this. . . ." Windy said.

Before long, Luke and Windy were surrounded by a group of scavenging Jawas! The strange little creatures combed the desert in search of junk—old ships and scrap metal—which they fixed up and sold to the Tatooine settlers. And right now they were after Luke's T-16!

"Hey! Get away from there!" Luke shouted.

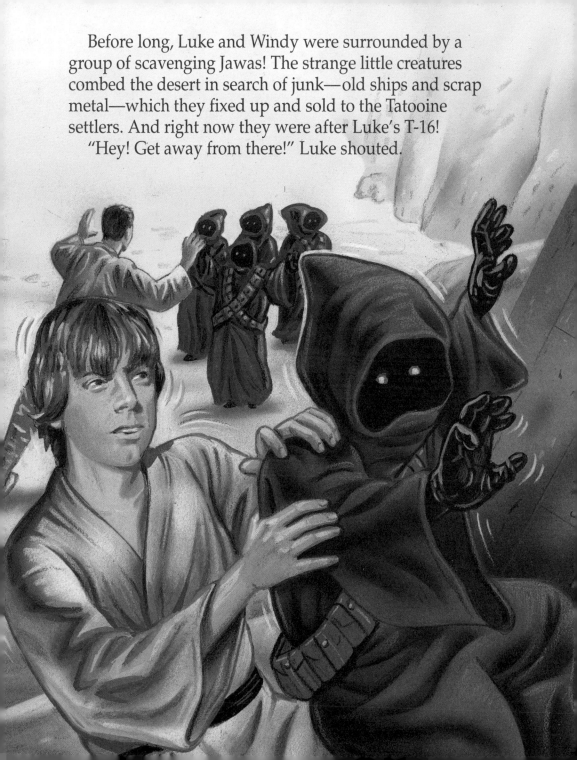

With lots of shouts and arm waving, Luke and Windy finally chased
away the Jawas. But soon after, more dangerous visitors arrived.

"Sand People!" Luke exclaimed worriedly. "We better hide!"

Luke and Windy hurried behind a large boulder. Peeking out from
their hiding place, they saw a band of the nasty-looking nomads climb
off their giant, hairy banthas and approach the T-16.

Then one of the Sand People began searching for survivors!
Luke and Windy held their breath as the nomad passed
their hiding place—and kept on going! *Whew!*

By the time the Sand People climbed on their banthas and
rode away, it was getting dark.

"We'd better make camp," Luke said.

Luckily, the Sand People hadn't found the blankets or
lantern Luke kept hidden in the T-16. Luke pulled them out,
while Windy found a cave-like spot for their camp.

Just then, a terrible roar echoed off the canyon walls.
"A krayt dragon!" Windy whispered as his eyes went wide.
Luke looked around nervously. Krayt dragons were the
fiercest animals on Tatooine. They attacked almost anything!

Suddenly, one of the terrifying beasts rushed out of the
darkness—straight at them!

Panicked, Luke and Windy looked for an escape. But
the canyon rose straight up behind them, and the dragon
blocked the path in front of them. They were trapped!

At that moment, a mysterious figure appeared out of the darkness—a man in a hooded robe.

In a simple gesture, the figure held his hand up in front of the dragon. Strangely, the dragon reared up fearfully, then scurried into the darkness.

"Who are you?" Luke asked.

"My name is Ben," the man replied. "I live in the Jundland Wastes."

"How did you do that?" Windy asked, still amazed by the dragon's departure.

Ben smiled. "You two had better get some sleep," he said. "We have a long day in front of us if we're going to get you two back home."

Early the next morning, the threesome started the long journey to Luke's uncle's farm. Before long, they came across a herd of wild dewbacks. Windy looked worried, but Luke noticed that Ben was staring at one of the big creatures. A second later, it walked right up to them!

Riding the dewback, Luke, Windy, and Ben soon
arrived at the moisture farm. Luke was relieved
to be home and excited to tell his aunt and uncle
about how Ben had saved them.

After hugging his aunt and uncle, Luke launched into the story. "It was amazing!" he said. But then he noticed that Uncle Owen seemed to recognize Ben. Could they know each other?

Luke turned to Ben, but he was already off in the distance. He disappeared into the desert landscape as quickly as he'd appeared in Beggar's Canyon the night before!

The next day, Luke and Windy took lots of tools and headed back out to Beggar's Canyon in Luke's landspeeder.

As Luke bent over the skyhopper's engine and got to work, Ben popped into his mind. It almost felt as though Ben was watching over him, and would always be with him. . . .